For everyone who
believes in fairies

Special thanks to
Sue Bentley

ORCHARD BOOKS
338 Euston Road, London NW1 3BH
Orchard Books Australia
Level 17/207 Kent Street, Sydney, NSW 2000
A Paperback Original

First published in 2003 by Orchard Books.

© 2008 Rainbow Magic Limited.
A HIT Entertainment company. Rainbow Magic
is a trademark of Rainbow Magic Limited.
Reg. U.S. Pat. & Tm. Off. And other countries.

HiT entertainment

Illustrations © Georgie Ripper 2003

A CIP catalogue record for this book is available
from the British Library.

ISBN 978 1 84362 020 4
33

Printed in Great Britain

Orchard Books is a division of Hachette Children's Books,
an Hachette Livre UK company

www.hachettelivre.co.uk

Sky
the Blue
Fairy

by Daisy Meadows

illustrated by Georgie Ripper

ORCHARD BOOKS

Cold winds blow and thick ice form,
I conjure up this fairy storm.
To seven corners of the mortal world
the Rainbow Fairies will be hurled!

I curse every part of Fairyland,
with a frosty wave of my icy hand.
For now and always, from this fateful day,
Fairyland will be cold and grey!

Ruby, Amber, Saffron and Fern
have been found. Now Rachel
and Kirsty must seek out
Sky the **Blue Fairy**

Contents

A Magic Messenger   9

Bubble Trouble   21

Goblins on Ice   29

Little Crab's Great Idea   43

Back to the Pot!   53

The Fairy Ring   61

A Magic Messenger

"The water's really warm!" laughed Rachel Walker. She was sitting on a rock, swishing her toes in one of Rainspell Island's deep, blue rock pools. Her friend Kirsty Tate was looking for shells on the rocks nearby.

"Mind you don't slip, Kirsty!" called Mrs Tate. She was sitting further down the beach with Mrs Walker.

"OK, Mum!" Kirsty yelled back. As she looked down at her bare feet, a patch of green seaweed began to move. There was something blue and shiny underneath it. "Rachel! Come over here," she shouted.

Rachel went over to Kirsty. "What
is it?" she asked.

Kirsty pointed to the seaweed. "There's
something blue under there," she said.
"I wonder, could it be…"

"Sky the Blue Fairy?" Rachel said
eagerly.

Jack Frost had banished the seven
Rainbow Fairies from Fairyland with a
magic spell. Now they were hidden on
Rainspell Island. Until they were all found
there would be no colour in Fairyland.
Rachel and Kirsty had promised the Fairy
King and Queen to help find them.

The seaweed twitched.

Rachel felt her heart beat faster.
"Maybe the fairy is all tangled up," she
whispered. "Like Fern when she landed
on the ivy in the tower."

Fern was the Green Rainbow Fairy. Rachel and Kirsty had already found Fern and her sisters Ruby, Amber and Saffron.

Suddenly a crab scuttled out from under the seaweed. It was bright blue and very shiny. Tiny rainbows sparkled across its shell. It didn't look like any of the other crabs on the beach.

Red, orange, yellow, green, blue, indigo and violet.

Kirsty and Rachel smiled at each other. This must be more of Rainspell Island's special magic!

"Oh no! Fairy in trouble!" the crab muttered in a tiny voice. It sounded a bit like two pebbles rubbing together.

"Did you hear that?" Rachel gasped.

The crab stopped and peered up at the girls with his little stalk eyes. Then he stood up on his back legs.

"What's he doing?" Kirsty said in surprise.

The crab pointed a claw towards some rocks further along under the cliffs. He scuttled away for a few steps, then came back and looked up at Rachel and Kirsty again. "Over there," he said in his scratchy voice.

"I think he wants us to follow him," Rachel said.

"Yes! Yes!" said the little crab, clicking his claws. He set off sideways across a large flat rock.

Kirsty turned to Rachel. "Perhaps he knows where Sky is!"

"I hope so," Rachel replied, her eyes shining.

The crab scuttled across a stretch of sand. Rachel and Kirsty followed him. It was a hot, sunny day. Seagulls flew overhead on strong, white wings.

"Rachel, Kirsty, it's nearly lunchtime!" called Mrs Walker. "We're going back to Dolphin Cottage."

Kirsty looked at Rachel in dismay.
"But we have to stay here and look for
the Blue Fairy. What shall we do?"

The little crab jumped up and
down, kicking up tiny puffs
of sand. "Follow me,
follow me!" he said.

Rachel thought
quickly. "Mum?" she
called back. "Could
we have a picnic
here instead, please?"

Mrs Walker smiled.
"Why not? It's a
beautiful day. And we should
make the most of the last three days
of our holiday. I'll pop back to the
cottage with Kirsty's mum and fetch
some sandwiches."

Only three days, thought Kirsty, and three Rainbow Fairies still to find: Sky, Izzy, and Heather!

The two girls waved as their mums left. Kirsty turned to Rachel. "We'd better hurry. They'll be back soon."

The crab set off again over a big slippery rock. Rachel and Kirsty climbed carefully after him. Rachel saw him stop by a small pool. There were lots of pretty pink shells in it.

"Is the fairy in one of the rock pools?" she asked. "Is it this one?"

The crab looked into the pool. He scratched the top of his head with one claw, looking puzzled. Then he scuttled away.

"I guess not," Kirsty said.

"What about here?" Rachel said, stopping by another pool. This one had tiny silver fish swimming in it. But the crab shook his claw at them and kept going.

"Not this one either," said Kirsty.

Suddenly Rachel spotted a large pool. It was all by itself, right at the foot of the cliff. "Let's try that one," she said, pointing.

Kirsty ran over.

The sky was reflected in the surface of the pool like a shiny, blue mirror.

Rachel caught up with her friend. She leaned over and looked into the water.

The crab scuttled up behind them, his stalk eyes waggling like mad. When he dipped his claw into the pool, the water fizzed like lemonade.

"Fairy!" cried the little crab, lifting his claw out of the water. Blue sparkles dripped off it and landed in the pool with a sizzle. The entire pool was shimmering with magic!

Bubble Trouble

"Thank you, little crab," Rachel said. She crouched down and stroked the top of the crab's shell.

The crab waved one claw at her, then dived into the water. He sank to the sandy bottom and scuttled out of sight under some seaweed.

Kirsty peered into the pool. "Can you

see the Blue Fairy?" she asked.

Rachel shook her head.

Kirsty felt disappointed. "I can't either."

"Do you think Jack Frost's goblins have found her?" Rachel said.

"I hope not!" Kirsty shuddered. "They'll do anything to stop the Rainbow Fairies getting back to Fairyland."

Just then, Rachel and Kirsty heard a sweet voice singing a song. "With silver bells and cockle shells, and pretty maids all in a row..."

"Oh!" Rachel gasped. "Do you think it's the little crab?"

Kirsty shook her head. "His voice was all gritty."

"You're right," Rachel agreed. "This sounds tinkly – more like a fairy!"

"I think the singing is coming from that seaweed," said Kirsty, pointing into the rock pool.

Rachel peered right in. She could see something unusual in the rippling water. "Look!" she said.

A huge bubble came bobbing out of the seaweed. It floated towards the surface of the pool.

Rachel and Kirsty watched, their eyes very wide. There was a tiny girl inside the bubble! She waved at them and fluttered her rainbow-coloured wings.

"Oh!" Kirsty gasped. "I think we've found Sky the Blue Fairy!"

The fairy pressed her hands against
the curved sides of the bubble. She wore
a short, sparkly dress and knee-high
boots the colour of bluebells. Her
earrings and hairband were made of
tiny stars, and she was holding a silver
wand.

"Please help me!" Sky said in a tiny
voice like bubbles popping.

Suddenly, a cold breeze stirred Rachel's
hair. A dark shadow fell across the pool.
The glowing blue water turned grey. It
was as if a cloud had covered the sun.

Rachel looked up. The sun was still
shining brightly overhead. "What's
happening?" she cried.

Kirsty heard a strange hissing,
crackling sound. She glanced
around in alarm.

A layer of frost was creeping across the
rocks towards them, covering the beach
in a crisp, white blanket.

"Jack Frost's goblins must be very near," Kirsty said, feeling worried.

In her bubble, Sky shivered, as ice began to cover the pool.

"Oh, no! She's going to be trapped," Kirsty gasped.

Sky's bubble had stopped bobbing. Now it hung very still, frozen into the ice. Sky looked very scared.

"Poor Sky! We have to rescue her!"
Rachel exclaimed. "But how can we
melt all that ice?"

"I know!" said Kirsty. "Why don't
we look in our magic bags?"

The Fairy Queen had given Rachel
and Kirsty bags with very special gifts
in them, to use for helping fairies in
trouble.

"Of course!" Rachel said. Then she
frowned. "Oh, no! I've left them in
my rucksack on the other side of the
rock pools!"

Goblins on Ice

"I'll run back and fetch the magic bags," Rachel said, jumping quickly to her feet.

"OK," Kirsty said. She blew on her hands to warm them. The frost was making the air chilly. "I'll stay here. But hurry!"

"I won't be long," Rachel promised.

She scrambled back over the rocks and on to the sandy beach.

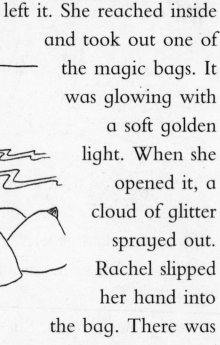

Her rucksack was lying where she'd left it. She reached inside and took out one of the magic bags. It was glowing with a soft golden light. When she opened it, a cloud of glitter sprayed out. Rachel slipped her hand into the bag. There was something there, smooth and shiny like a pebble. She pulled it out and looked closely at it. It was a tiny blue stone, shaped a bit like a raindrop.

Rachel felt very puzzled. It was pretty but how could it help?

Then the blue stone began to glow in her hand, hotter and hotter until it was almost too warm to hold. As it grew hotter, it glowed fiery red. Rachel curled her fingers around the raindrop stone in delight. They could use it to melt the ice and set Sky free!

She ran back as fast as she could. But when she reached the rocks, she stopped dead. Kirsty was still standing by Sky's frozen pool, but she wasn't on her own any more. Two ugly hook-nosed goblins were skating on the ice beside her!

"Shoo! Go away!" Kirsty was shouting at them, waving her hands.

Rachel could tell that Kirsty was really angry. Rachel didn't feel quite so scared either, now she'd brought fairy magic to help fight the goblins.

"Go away yourself!" yelled one of the goblins rudely at Kirsty. He held his stumpy arms out sideways and slid across the ice on one foot away from her.

Kirsty tried to grab the other goblin. But he dodged, out of reach. "Can't catch me!"

"Hee, hee! The fairy can't get out!" the other goblin laughed. His bulging eyes gleamed as he did a little twirl.

"We're *going* to get her out!" Kirsty told him. "We're going to find *all* the Rainbow Fairies. And then Fairyland will get its colours back!"

"Oh no, it won't," said the goblin.
He stuck out his tongue and screwed
up his nose.

"Jack Frost's magic is too strong,"
said the other goblin. "Hey, look at
me!" He pointed one foot out behind
him and whizzed round the pool. But
the ice was very slippery. He skidded
sideways and crashed right into his
friend.

Splat!

"Clumsy!" the goblin snapped crossly.

"You should have moved out of the
way," grumbled the other one, rubbing
his bottom.

The goblins tried to stand up. But
their feet skidded in all directions and
they fell over again in a heap. Rachel
saw her chance. She ran to the edge of
the pool and threw the magic
blue stone on to the ice.

Suddenly, there was a *fizz* and a
bang! A shower of golden sparks shot
into the air and the ice began to melt.
A big hole appeared in the centre of
the pool.

"Ow! Hot! Hot!" yelled the goblins, slithering about on the ice. They scrambled to the edge of the pool and rushed away, their big feet slapping on the rocks.

"They've gone!" Kirsty said in relief. Rachel peered into the pool. "I hope Sky isn't hurt," she said.

All the ice had melted and the water reflected the blue sky once again. Sky's bubble was floating just below the surface.

Rachel saw Sky sit up inside the bubble and look around. Her eyes were big and scared, and she looked very pale.

Kirsty put her hand in the water. It was still warm from the magic stone. "Don't be afraid, Sky," she said. Very gently, she poked her finger into the bubble.

Pop!

Sky tumbled free of the bubble and into the water. She swam up to the surface, her golden hair streaming behind her.

Kirsty leaned over and fished the fairy out. She felt like a tiny wet leaf. Kirsty placed her gently on a rock in the sun. "There you are, little fairy," she whispered.

Sky propped herself up on one elbow. Water dripped from her everywhere, but there were no blue sparkles now. "Thank you for helping me," she said in a weak voice.

Kirsty frowned at Rachel. "Something's wrong. All the fairies we found before had fairy dust. What has happened to Sky's sparkles?"

"I don't know," said Rachel. "And she's gone really pale, almost white."

It was true. Sky's dress was so pale, you could hardly tell it was blue at all.

Kirsty bit her lip. "It looks as if Jack Frost's magic has taken away her colour!"

The blue crab scuttled out of the water and made his way across the rock to Sky. "Oh dear, oh dear," he muttered. "Poor little fairy."

Sky shivered and wrapped her arms around herself. "I'm so cold and sleepy," she whispered.

Kirsty felt a pang of alarm. "What's the matter, Sky? Did the goblins get too close to you?"

Sky nodded weakly. "Yes, and now I can't get warm."

"We've got to help her," Rachel said.

"But how?" asked Kirsty. She looked down in dismay at Sky, curled up in a tiny ball with her eyes closed.

Rachel felt tears prick behind her
eyelids.

Poor Sky. She looked really ill. What
was going to happen to her?

Little Crab's Great Idea

Rachel spotted something moving. The little blue crab was waggling his front claws madly. "Look!" she said.

"He's trying to tell us something," said Kirsty.

The girls crouched down.

"Don't worry," the crab said in his gritty voice. "My friends will help us."

He scuttled up to the top of the highest
rock and snapped his claws.

"What's he going to do?" Kirsty
wondered. Then she stared in
amazement.

Lots and lots of crabs were coming
out of the rock pools around them. Big
ones, little ones, all different colours.
Their claws made scratchy noises on
the pebbles.

The blue crab wiggled his eyes and clicked his claws, pointing up at the sky, then down at the ground. His friends pattered away in all directions. Their little stalk eyes waved about as they prodded their claws into the cracks between the rocks.

Rachel and Kirsty looked at each other, feeling very confused. "What's going on?" said Rachel.

Just then, Kirsty spotted a tiny pink
crab tugging and tugging
at something. With a
gritty crunch, the
crab tumbled over
backwards. It
held a fluffy white
seagull feather in
its claws. The crab
scrambled up again,
waving the feather in the air.

One by one, the other crabs searched
out more feathers. Then the blue crab
waved them over to the rock where
Sky lay. Very carefully he tucked the
feathers round the Blue Fairy. His
friends brought more and more
feathers, until the fairy was lying in
a cosy feather bed.

"They're trying to warm Sky up with seagull feathers!" Kirsty said.

Rachel held her breath. There were so many feathers now that she couldn't see the fairy at all. Would the blue crab's idea work? she wondered.

There was the tiniest wriggle in the feather nest. A faint puff of blue sparkles fizzed up, smelling of blueberries. One pale blue star wobbled upwards and disappeared with a pop.

"Fairy dust!" Rachel whispered.

"Mmmm... But there's not very much of it," Kirsty pointed out.

There was another wriggle from inside the nest. The feathers fell apart to reveal the Blue Fairy, her dress still very pale. She opened her big, blue eyes and sat up.

"Hello, I'm Sky the Blue Fairy. Who are you?" she said in a sleepy voice.

"I'm Kirsty," said Kirsty.

"And I'm Rachel," said Rachel.

"Thank you for frightening the goblins away," said Sky. "And thank you, little crab, for finding all these lovely, warm feathers." She tried to unfold her wings, but they were too crumpled.

"My poor wings," said the fairy, her eyes filling with tiny tears.

"The feathers have helped, but Sky still can't fly," Kirsty said.

"Maybe the other Rainbow Fairies can help," Rachel said.

Sky looked up excitedly. "Do you know where my sisters are?" she asked.

"Oh, yes," said Kirsty. "So far, we've found Ruby, Amber, Saffron, and Fern."

"They are safe in the pot-at-the-end-of-the-rainbow," Rachel added.

"Could you take me to them,
please?" said Sky. "I'm sure they will
make me better." She tried to stand up,
but her legs were too wobbly and she
had to sit down again.

"Here, let me carry you," Rachel
offered. She cupped her hands and
scooped up the feather nest with the
fairy inside.

Sky waved at the little blue crab and
his friends. "Goodbye. Thank you
again for helping me."

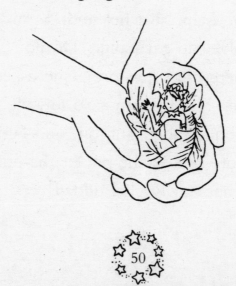

"Goodbye, goodbye!" The blue crab
waved his claw. His friends waved too,
their little stalk eyes shining proudly.
They had never rescued a Rainbow
Fairy before.

Kirsty and Rachel glanced at each
other as they crunched across the pebbles.
Sky was being very brave, but the
goblins had got closer to her than any of
the other Rainbow Fairies. And now the
Blue Fairy was hardly blue at all!

Back to the Pot!

Rachel and Kirsty hurried across the fields and into the woods. Rachel carried Sky very carefully. The fairy lay curled in a ball in the warm feathers, her cheek resting on her pale hands.

"Here's the glade with the willow tree," Kirsty said.

The scent of oranges hung in the
air, tickling their noses. Rachel looked
round and spotted a tiny fairy. She
was hovering over a patch of daisies,
collecting nectar in an acorn cup.

"Look!" Rachel said. "It's Amber the
Orange Fairy."

"Hello again, Rachel and Kirsty!"
Amber fluttered over and settled on
Rachel's shoulder.

Then Amber saw Sky lying curled up
in Rachel's hand. "Oh, no! Sky, what's
happened? I must call the others,"

she cried. She waved
her wand and
a fountain of
sparkling orange
dust shot into
the air.

The other Rainbow Fairies fluttered up all over the clearing. The air sparkled with red, orange, yellow, and green fairy dust. Bubbles and flowers, tiny butterflies and leaves sprinkled the grass.

Rachel and Kirsty watched as the fairies clustered around Sky. The Blue Fairy sat up slightly and gave a weak smile, then flopped back into her nest of feathers.

"Oh, Sky!" cried Fern, the gentle Green Fairy.

"Why is she so pale?" Saffron asked.

"The goblins got really close to her," Rachel explained. "They froze the pond. Sky was trapped in a bubble under the ice."

"Ooooh! That's terrible." Saffron shuddered.

"Kirsty shouted at them and tried to catch them," Sky whispered.

"Thank you. You are so brave!" said

Ruby the Red Fairy, then she zoomed high into the air. "We must think of something to help Sky! Oh, I know! Let's ask Bertram for his advice!"

The fairy sisters sped towards the willow tree, their wings flashing brightly. Rachel and Kirsty carried Sky over in her feathery nest.

The pot-at-the-end-of-the-rainbow lay on its side underneath the willow's trailing branches. The Rainbow Fairies were living there until all their sisters had been found, and they could go back to Fairyland.

As Rachel put Sky down beside the pot, a large green frog hopped out.

"Miss Sky!" he croaked, looking pleased.

"Hello, Bertram." Sky gave another weak smile.

"We have to make Sky warm so she gets her colour back," Fern explained.

Bertram looked very worried. "Jack Frost's goblins are so cruel," he said. "You must stay close to the pot, Fairies, so that I can protect you."

"Don't worry," said Saffron, giving Sky a hug. "You'll soon feel better."

Sky nodded, but she didn't answer. Her eyes started to close. She was so pale, her arms and legs seemed almost transparent.

Rachel and Kirsty watched the Rainbow Fairies exchange worried glances. "Oh Bertram, what if the goblins have hurt Sky for ever!" exclaimed Fern. "What can we do to save her?"

The Fairy Ring

Bertram looked very serious. "I think it's time for you all to try a spell."

Amber frowned. "It might not work with only four of us. Rainbow Magic needs seven fairies!"

"Bertram's right, we have to try," Ruby said. "Perhaps we can manage a *small* spell. Quick, let's make a fairy ring."

The Rainbow Fairies fluttered into
a circle above Sky.

Rachel noticed a black-and-
yellow queen bee and a
small grey squirrel
appear at the edge
of the glade.
"Queenie and
Fluffy have come
to watch the
spell," she
whispered to
Kirsty. Queenie
the bee had
helped Saffron to
get her wand back
after the goblins stole it.
Fluffy the squirrel had
carried Fern and the girls back

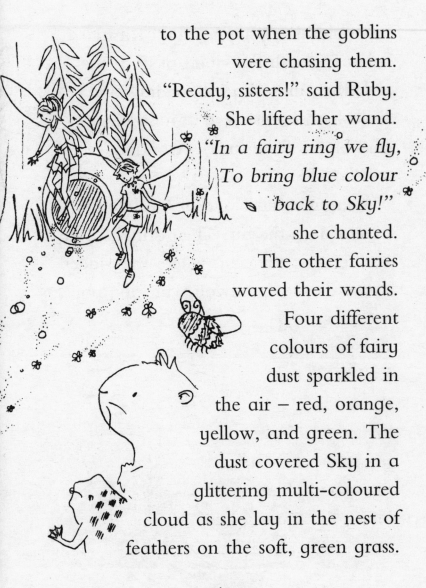

to the pot when the goblins were chasing them.

"Ready, sisters!" said Ruby. She lifted her wand. *"In a fairy ring we fly, To bring blue colour back to Sky!"* she chanted.

The other fairies waved their wands. Four different colours of fairy dust sparkled in the air – red, orange, yellow, and green. The dust covered Sky in a glittering multi-coloured cloud as she lay in the nest of feathers on the soft, green grass.

"Something's happening!" Kirsty
said. Through the cloud of dust, she
could see that Sky's short dress and
knee-high boots were turning bluer
and bluer. "The spell is working!"
Whoosh!
A shimmering cloud of blue stars
shot into the air. They drifted up to
the sky, where they faded
away with tiny pops.

"We did it!" cheered Amber, turning a cartwheel in the air, as Saffron clapped her hands in delight.

"Hooray for Rainbow Magic!" laughed Ruby.

Sky yawned and sat up. She brushed the feathers away and looked down at herself. Her face lit up. Her dress was blue again! "My wings feel strong enough to fly now," she said. She flapped them twice, then zoomed into the air. She did a twirl, her wings flashing with rainbows. "Thank you, sisters!"

The Rainbow Fairies clustered round Sky, hugging and kissing her. The air around them bubbled with fairy dust – red, orange, yellow, green and blue. It was nearly a whole rainbow!

Rachel and Kirsty beamed.

Fern swooped down and scooped
up an armful of seagull feathers.
"You won't need these any
more!" she laughed, tickling
Sky with a long, white one.

"But I think I might know what to
do with them!" said Sky. She flew
down to perch on the edge of the pot
and peeked in. "It's so cosy!" she said,
admiring the tiny chairs and tables
made of twigs, and the giant shell bed.

Then Sky fluttered over to the rest of
the feathers and gathered them up. "I
thought we could put these on our bed.
They'll be very warm and soft."

Her fairy sisters looked delighted.
"Thank you, Sky. What a good idea,"
said Ruby.

"Let's have a welcome home feast,"
said Fern. "With wild strawberries and
clover juice."

Amber did another cartwheel.
"Yippee! Rachel and Kirsty, you're
invited too!"

"Thank you, but we have to go."
Rachel looked at her watch. "Our
mums will be waiting with our
picnic."

"Oh, yes!" Kirsty remembered,
jumping up. She felt a bit disappointed
that she wouldn't have a chance to
taste some fairy food. But she didn't
want her mum to be worried.
"Goodbye, we'll be back again soon!"

The fairies sat on the edge of the pot
and waved to the girls. Queenie, Fluffy,
and Bertram the frog waved too.
"Goodbye! Goodbye!"

Sky fluttered beside Rachel and Kirsty as they walked back across the glade. Tiny rainbows sparkled on her wings. Her dress and boots glowed bright blue, and blueberry scent filled the air.

"Thank you so much, Rachel and Kirsty," she said. "Now five Rainbow Fairies are safe."

"We'll find Izzy and Heather too," Kirsty said. "I promise."

"Yes," Rachel agreed.

As they made their way back to the beach, Rachel looked at Kirsty. "Do you think we can find them in time? We only have two days of holiday left. And the goblins are getting much closer. They nearly caught Sky today!"

Kirsty squeezed her friend's hand and smiled. "Don't worry. Nothing is going to stop us from keeping our promise to the Rainbow Fairies!"

RAINBOW magic

Ruby, Amber, Saffron, Fern
and Sky are safe at last.
But where is
Izzy the Indigo Fairy?

A Fairytale Beginning

"Rain, rain, go away," Rachel Walker sighed. "Come again another day!"

She and her friend Kirsty Tate stared out of the attic window. Raindrops splashed against the glass, and the sky was full of purply-black clouds.

"Isn't it a horrible day?" Kirsty said. "But it's nice and cosy in here."

She looked round Rachel's small attic bedroom. There was just room for a brass bed with a patchwork quilt, a comfy armchair and an old bookcase.

"You know what the weather on

Rainspell is like," Rachel pointed out. "It might be hot and sunny very soon!"

Both girls had come to Rainspell Island on holiday. The Walkers were staying in Mermaid Cottage, while the Tates were in Dolphin Cottage next door.

Kirsty frowned. "Yes, but what about Izzy the Indigo Fairy?" she asked. "We have to find her today."

Rachel and Kirsty shared a wonderful secret. They were trying to find the seven Rainbow Fairies who had been cast out of Fairyland by evil Jack Frost. Fairyland would be cold and grey until all seven fairies had been found again.

Rachel thought of Ruby, Amber, Saffron, Fern and Sky, who were all safe now in the pot-at-the-end-of-the-rainbow. They only had Izzy the Indigo Fairy and Heather the Violet Fairy left to find. But how could they look for them while they were stuck indoors?

"Remember what the Fairy Queen said?" she reminded Kirsty.

Kirsty nodded. "She said the magic would come to us." Suddenly she looked scared. "Maybe the rain is Jack Frost's magic. Maybe he's trying to stop us finding Izzy."

"Oh no!" Rachel said. "Let's hope it stops soon. But what shall we do while we're waiting?"

Kirsty thought for a moment. Then she went over to the bookcase. It was filled with dusty, old books, and she pulled one out. It was so big, she had to use two hands to hold it.

"The Big Book of Fairy Tales," Rachel read out, looking at the cover.

"If we can't find fairies, at least we can read about them!" Kirsty grinned.

The two girls sat down on the bed and put the book on their knees. Kirsty was about to turn the first page when Rachel gasped. "Kirsty, look at the cover! It's purple. A really deep bluey-purple."

"That's indigo," Kirsty whispered. "Oh, Rachel! Do you think Izzy could be trapped inside?"

"Let's see," Rachel said. "Hurry up, Kirsty. Open the book!"

But Kirsty had spotted something else. "Rachel," she said shakily. "It's *glowing.*"

Rachel looked. Kirsty was right. Some pages in the middle of the book were gleaming with a soft bluey-purple light.

Kirsty opened the book. The ink on the pages was glowing indigo. For a moment Kirsty thought that Izzy might fly out of the pages, but there was no sign of her. On the first page was a picture of a wooden soldier. Above the picture were the words: *The Nutcracker.*

"Oh!" Rachel said. "I know this story. I went to see the ballet at Christmas."

"What's it about?" Kirsty asked.

"Well, a girl called Clara gets a wooden nutcracker soldier for Christmas," Rachel explained. "He comes to life and takes her to the Land of Sweets." They looked down at a brightly-coloured picture of a Christmas tree. A little girl was asleep beside it, holding a wooden soldier.

On the next page there was a picture of snowflakes whirling and swirling through a dark forest. "Aren't the pictures great?" Kirsty said. "The snow looks so real."

Rachel frowned. For a moment, she thought the snowflakes were moving. Gently she put out her hand and touched the page. It felt cold and wet!

"Kirsty," she whispered. "It *is* real!" She held out her hand. There were white snowflakes on her fingers.

Kirsty looked down at the book again, her eyes wide. The snowflakes started to swirl from the book's pages, right into the bedroom, slowly at first, then faster and faster.

Read the rest of

RAINBOW
magic
Izzy the Indigo Fairy

to find out what magic the swirling
snowstorm brings with it.

Win Rainbow Magic Goodies!

There are lots of Rainbow Magic fairies, and we want to know
which one is your favourite! Send us a picture of her and tell
us in thirty words why she is your favourite and why you like
Rainbow Magic books. Each month we will put the entries into
a draw and select one winner to receive a Rainbow Magic
Sparkly T-shirt and Goody Bag!

Send your entry on a postcard to Rainbow Magic Competition,
Orchard Books, 338 Euston Road, London NW1 3BH.
Australian readers should email: childrens.books@hachette.com.au
New Zealand readers should write to Rainbow Magic Competition,
4 Whetu Place, Mairangi Bay, Auckland NZ.
Don't forget to include your name and address.
Only one entry per child.

Good luck!